For my parents

First published 1988 by Walker Books Ltd
87 Vauxhall Walk, London SE11 5HJ

This edition published 2016

24 26 28 30 29 27 25

© 1987 – 2016 Martin Handford

The right of Martin Handford to be identified as author/illustrator
of this work has been asserted by him in accordance with the
Copyright, Designs and Patents Act 1988.

This book has been typeset in Wallyfont and Optima.

Printed in China

British Library Cataloguing in Publication Data:
a catalogue record for this book
is available from the British Library.

ISBN 978-1-4063-0586-9

www.walker.co.uk

WHERE'S WALLY NOW?

MARTIN HANDFORD

WALKER BOOKS
AND SUBSIDIARIES

LONDON • BOSTON • SYDNEY • AUCKLAND

HI THERE, BOOK WORMS!

SOME BITS OF HISTORY ARE AMAZING! I SIT HERE READING ALL THESE BOOKS ABOUT THE WORLD LONG AGO, AND IT'S LIKE RIDING A TIME MACHINE. WHY NOT TRY IT FOR YOURSELVES? JUST SEARCH EACH PICTURE AND FIND ME, WOOF (REMEMBER, ALL YOU CAN SEE IS HIS TAIL), WENDA, WIZARD WHITEBEARD AND ODLAW. THEN LOOK FOR MY KEY, WOOF'S BONE (IN THIS SCENE IT'S THE BONE THAT'S NEAREST TO HIS TAIL), WENDA'S CAMERA, WIZARD WHITEBEARD'S SCROLL AND ODLAW'S BINOCULARS.

THERE ARE ALSO 25 WALLY-WATCHERS, EACH OF WHOM APPEARS ONLY ONCE SOMEWHERE ON MY TRAVELS. AND ONE MORE THING! CAN YOU FIND ANOTHER CHARACTER, NOT SHOWN BELOW, WHO APPEARS ONCE IN EVERY PICTURE?

Wally

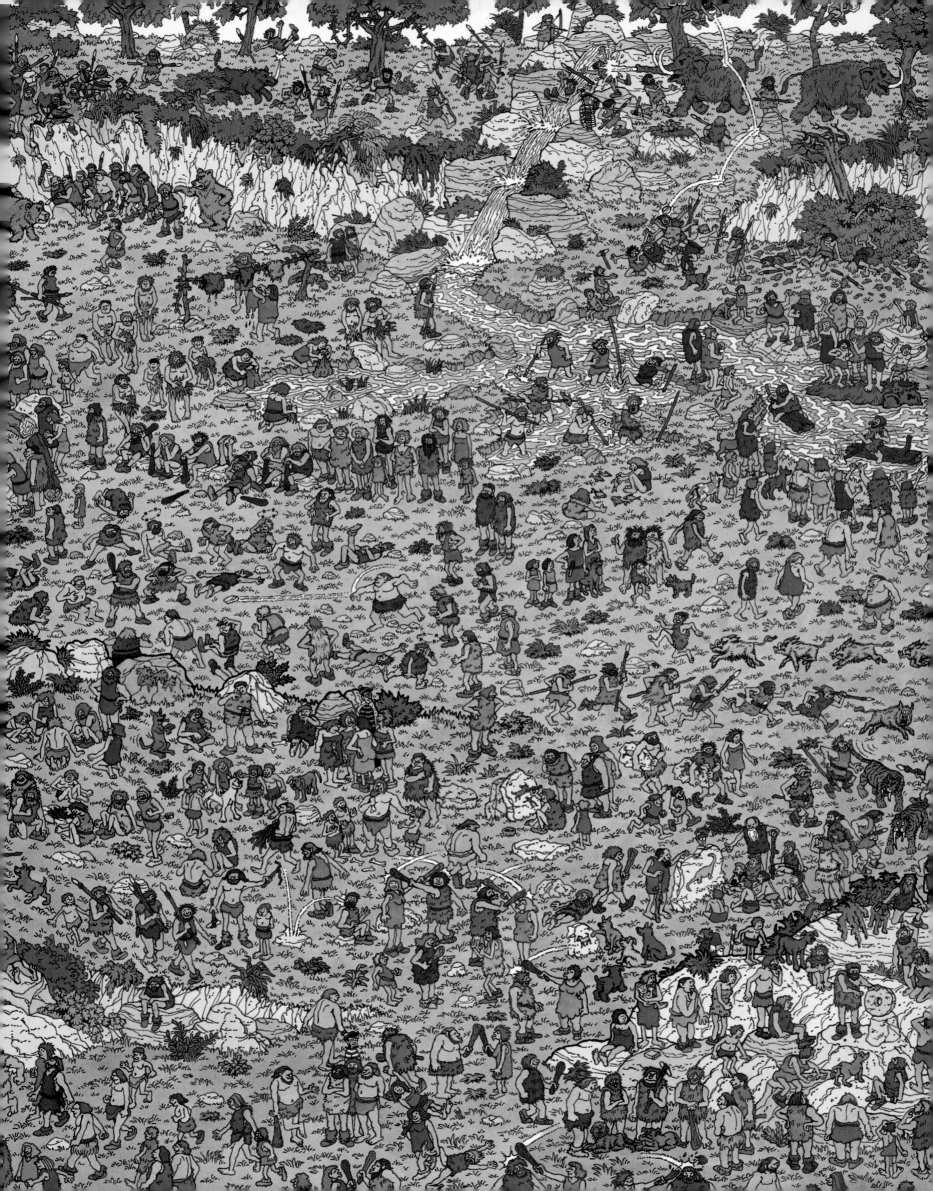

4,578 YEARS AGO

THE RIDDLE OF THE PYRAMIDS

THE ANCIENT EGYPTIANS WERE VERY CLEVER PEOPLE WHO LOVED GOATS, CATS AND SPHINXES, AND INVENTED PYRAMIDS. WITH GREAT SKILL AND HARD WORK THEY BUILT HUGE WONDERS IN THE DESERT.

BUT FOR HUNDREDS OF YEARS MANY PEOPLE WERE PUZZLED BY THEM. WHAT WERE THEY FOR? WHY WERE THEY SO BIG?

WHY WERE THEY THAT SHAPE? WAS IT POSSIBLE (OR EVEN LIKELY) THAT PHARAOHS WERE BURIED UNDER THEM? THESE MAGNIFICENT MONUMENTS ARE STILL AMAZING PEOPLE TO THIS DAY.

2,000 YEARS AGO

FVN AND GAMES IN ANCIENT ROME

THE ROMANS SPENT MOST OF THEIR TIME FIGHTING, CONQVERING, LEARNING LATIN AND MAKING ROADS. WHEN THEY TOOK THEIR HOLIDAYS THEY ALWAYS HAD GAMES AT THE COLISEVM (AN OLD SORT OF PLAYGROVND). THEIR FAVOURITE GAMES WERE FIGHTING, MORE FIGHTING, CHARIOT RACING, FIGHTING AND FEEDING CHRISTIANS TO LIONS. WHEN THE CROWD GAVE A GLADIATOR THE THVMBS DOWN, IT MEANT KILL YOUR OPPONENT. THVMBS UP MEANT LET HIM GO, TO FIGHT TO THE DEATH ANOTHER DAY.

ON TOUR WITH THE VIKINGS

At home the Vikings were quiet people, who liked knitting and cheese tasting and boring things like that. But on tour they went wild. They put on their best horned hats and sailed across the sea, singing and shouting like mad. If you heard them coming, it was best to run away because once they had arrived and unpacked their axes, there was no holding them back.

Chaos at the Castle

Castles were built all across Europe and the people living in them often had a beautiful view of the countryside. Unfortunately they might also have had a view of an army laying siege to their castle. Luckily when these besieging armies finally ran out of clean tights and tunics they returned home. For years afterwards the knights told stories of the spectacular castles they had battered and bashed and the fascinating people they had captured — and wondered why they were never invited to parties!

600 YEARS AGO

ONCE UPON A SATURDAY MORNING

The Middle Ages were a very merry time to be alive, especially on Saturdays, as long as you didn't get caught. Short skirts and stripy tights were in fashion for men; everybody knew lots of jokes; there was widespread juggling

and jousting and archery and jesting and fun. But if you got into trouble, the Middle Ages could be miserable. For the man in the stocks or the pillory or about to lose his head, Saturday morning was no laughing matter.

THE LAST DAYS OF THE AZTECS

The Aztecs lived in sunny Mexico and were rich and strong and liked swinging from poles pretending to be eagles. They also liked making human sacrifices to their gods, so it was best to agree with everything they said. The Spanish were also rich and strong, and some of them, called conquistadors, came to Mexico in 1519 to have an adventure.

However, when the Aztecs and Spanish met they did not agree on much.

400 YEARS AGO

Is red better than blue? What do you mean, your poem about cherry blossom is better than mine? Shall we have another cup of tea? Over difficult questions such as these, the Japanese fought fiercely for hundreds of years. The fiercest fighters of all were the samurai, who wore flags on their backs so that their mummies could find them. The fighters without flags were called ashigaru. They couldn't take a joke any better than the samurai, especially about not having flags.

TROUBLE IN OLD JAPAN

250 YEARS AGO

BEING A PIRATE
(Shiver-me-timbers!)

It was really a lot of fun being a pirate, especially if you were very hairy and didn't have much in the way of brains. It also helped if you had a peg-leg, an eye patch, a bandana and had a pirate's hat with your name-tag sewn inside and a treasure-map and a rusty cutlass. Once there were lots of pirates, but they died out in the end because too many of them were men (which is not a good idea).

HAVING A BALL

IN GAYE PAREE

The history of France has some very bad bits, like getting your head chopped off by Madame Guillotine in the French Revolution; and some very good bits, like the invention of smelly cheese. In 1870 Napoleon (the third one) threw a marvellous ball in Paris to celebrate 1870 being a good bit. All the beautiful people came and danced the night away to a band called the Third Republic.

100 YEARS AGO

THE GOLD RUSH

At the end of the 19th century large numbers of excited **AMERICANS** were frequently to be seen **RUSHING** headlong towards **HOLES** in the ground, hoping to find **GOLD**. Most of them never even found the holes in the ground. But at least they had a **GOOD DAY**, with plenty of **EXERCISE** and **FRESH AIR**, which kept them **HEALTHY**. And health is much more valuable than **GOLD** . . . well, nearly more valuable . . . isn't it?

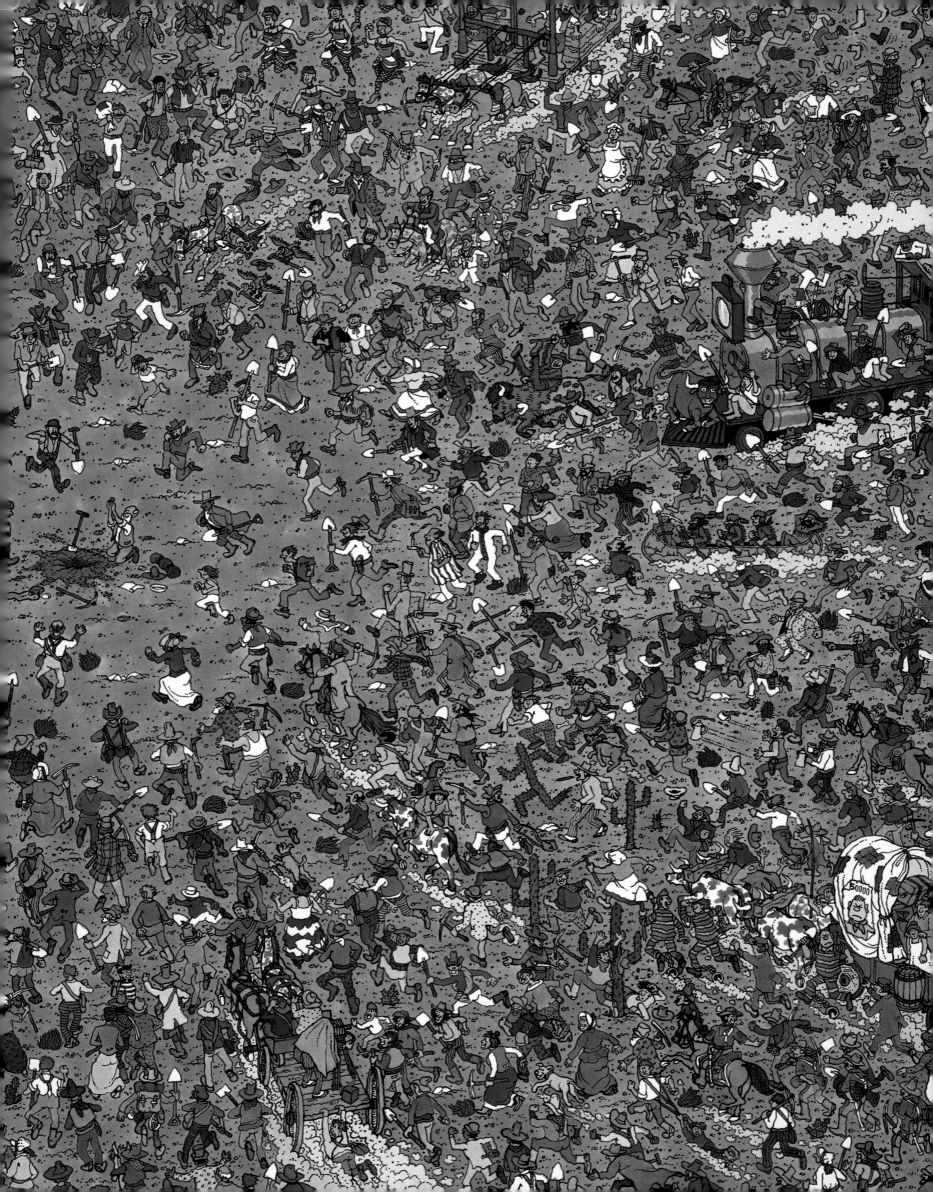

WALLY IS LOST
IN THE FUTURE!
FIND HIM! RESCUE HIM!
WALLY'S BOOKS ARE LOST
IN THE PAST!
FIND THEM! RESCUE THEM!
THERE'S ONE LOST IN EACH
PICTURE. GO BACK
AND LOOK FOR THEM!
WHERE'S WALLY?
WHERE'S WALLY
NOW?

THE GREAT WHERE'S WALLY NOW? CHECKLIST
Hundreds more things for time travellers to look for!

THE STONE AGE

- Four cavemen swinging into trouble
- An accident with an axe
- A great invention
- A Stone-Age rodeo
- Boars chasing a man
- Men chasing a boar
- Seven fish
- Romantic cavemen and cavewomen
- A mammoth squirt
- A bear trap
- A mammoth in the river
- A fruit stall
- Charging woolly rhinos
- A big cover-up
- A trunk holding a trunk
- A knock-out game of baseball
- A rocky picture show
- An upside-down boar
- A spoiled dog
- A lesson on dinosaurs
- A very scruffy family
- Some dangerous spear fishermen

FUN AND GAMES IN ANCIENT ROME

- A charioteer who has lost his chariot
- Coliseum cleaners
- An unequal contest with spears
- A winner who is about to lose
- A lion with good table manners
- A deadly set of wheels
- Lion cubs being teased
- Four shields that match their owners
- A leopard chasing a leopard skin
- Lions giving the paws-down
- A pyramid of lions
- A piggyback puncher
- An awful musician
- A painful fork-lift
- A horse holding the reins
- A leopard in love
- A Roman keeping score
- A gladiator losing his sandals

CHAOS AT THE CASTLE

- A soldier getting the point
- A man about to be catapulted
- A human bridge
- A key that is out of reach
- A message in a bottle
- A cauldron of boiling oil
- A battering-man
- Two hands gripping a soldier's arms
- A catapult aiming the wrong way
- Six defenders wearing red shoes
- A load of washing
- A shower of spears
- A soldier fast asleep
- A ladder that is too short
- Flattened soldiers
- Rock faces
- Attackers in the wrong colour stripes
- A ticklish situation

THE RIDDLE OF THE PYRAMIDS

- A Pharaoh choosing a sarcophagus
- An upside-down pyramid
- A little boy helping to paint a mural
- Someone wearing a red cape
- A chariot racer without his chariot
- Men carrying a mural in a mural
- A group of posing gods
- Six workers pushing a block of stone
- Two assistants mixing paint
- Dates falling from a tree
- Stones defying gravity
- A thirsty sphinx
- A runaway block of stone
- Nine shields
- Someone blowing a horn
- A picture firing an arrow
- Three water-carriers
- Sunbathers in peril
- A messy milking session
- A contented animal being petted
- Pyramids of sand

ON TOUR WITH THE VIKINGS

- A happy figurehead
- Figureheads in love
- A man being used as a club
- A tearful sheep
- Two hopeless hiding places
- Some childish Vikings
- Three spearheads being lopped off
- An eagle posing as a helmet
- A sailor tearing a sail
- A heavily armed Viking
- A patchy couple
- A beard with a foot on it
- A burning behind
- A bending boat
- Three startled figureheads
- Locked horns
- A helmet with a spider on it
- A helmet of smoke
- A bullfight

ONCE UPON A SATURDAY MORNING

- A dirty downpour
- Archers missing the target
- A jouster sitting back to front
- A dog stalking a cat stalking some birds
- A jouster who needs lots of practice
- A man making a bear dance
- A bear making a man dance
- Fruit and vegetable thieves
- Hats that are tied together
- A juggling jester
- A long line of pickpockets
- A very long drink
- A heavily burdened beast
- A gentleman kissing a lady's hand
- A man scything hats
- An angry fish
- A ticklish torture
- Minstrels making an awful noise

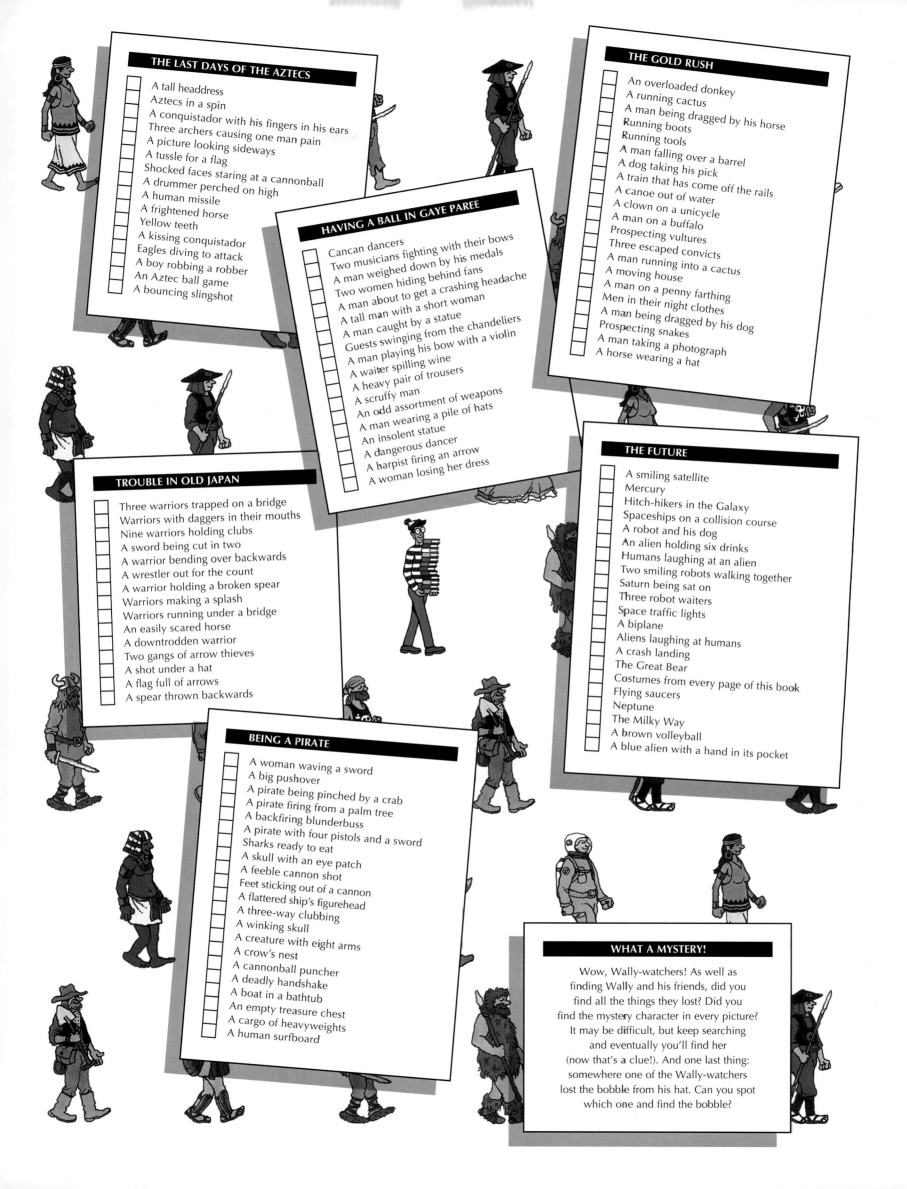

THE LAST DAYS OF THE AZTECS

- A tall headdress
- Aztecs in a spin
- A conquistador with his fingers in his ears
- Three archers causing one man pain
- A picture looking sideways
- A tussle for a flag
- Shocked faces staring at a cannonball
- A drummer perched on high
- A human missile
- A frightened horse
- Yellow teeth
- A kissing conquistador
- Eagles diving to attack
- A boy robbing a robber
- An Aztec ball game
- A bouncing slingshot

THE GOLD RUSH

- An overloaded donkey
- A running cactus
- A man being dragged by his horse
- Running boots
- Running tools
- A man falling over a barrel
- A dog taking his pick
- A train that has come off the rails
- A canoe out of water
- A clown on a unicycle
- A man on a buffalo
- Prospecting vultures
- Three escaped convicts
- A man running into a cactus
- A moving house
- A man on a penny farthing
- Men in their night clothes
- A man being dragged by his dog
- Prospecting snakes
- A man taking a photograph
- A horse wearing a hat

HAVING A BALL IN GAYE PAREE

- Cancan dancers
- Two musicians fighting with their bows
- A man weighed down by his medals
- Two women hiding behind fans
- A man about to get a crashing headache
- A tall man with a short woman
- A man caught by a statue
- Guests swinging from the chandeliers
- A man playing his bow with a violin
- A waiter spilling wine
- A heavy pair of trousers
- A scruffy man
- An odd assortment of weapons
- A man wearing a pile of hats
- An insolent statue
- A dangerous dancer
- A harpist firing an arrow
- A woman losing her dress

TROUBLE IN OLD JAPAN

- Three warriors trapped on a bridge
- Warriors with daggers in their mouths
- Nine warriors holding clubs
- A sword being cut in two
- A warrior bending over backwards
- A wrestler out for the count
- A warrior holding a broken spear
- Warriors making a splash
- Warriors running under a bridge
- An easily scared horse
- A downtrodden warrior
- Two gangs of arrow thieves
- A shot under a hat
- A flag full of arrows
- A spear thrown backwards

THE FUTURE

- A smiling satellite
- Mercury
- Hitch-hikers in the Galaxy
- Spaceships on a collision course
- A robot and his dog
- An alien holding six drinks
- Humans laughing at an alien
- Two smiling robots walking together
- Saturn being sat on
- Three robot waiters
- Space traffic lights
- A biplane
- Aliens laughing at humans
- A crash landing
- The Great Bear
- Costumes from every page of this book
- Flying saucers
- Neptune
- The Milky Way
- A brown volleyball
- A blue alien with a hand in its pocket

BEING A PIRATE

- A woman waving a sword
- A big pushover
- A pirate being pinched by a crab
- A pirate firing from a palm tree
- A backfiring blunderbuss
- A pirate with four pistols and a sword
- Sharks ready to eat
- A skull with an eye patch
- A feeble cannon shot
- Feet sticking out of a cannon
- A flattered ship's figurehead
- A three-way clubbing
- A winking skull
- A creature with eight arms
- A crow's nest
- A cannonball puncher
- A deadly handshake
- A boat in a bathtub
- An empty treasure chest
- A cargo of heavyweights
- A human surfboard

WHAT A MYSTERY!

Wow, Wally-watchers! As well as finding Wally and his friends, did you find all the things they lost? Did you find the mystery character in every picture? It may be difficult, but keep searching and eventually you'll find her (now that's a clue!). And one last thing: somewhere one of the Wally-watchers lost the bobble from his hat. Can you spot which one and find the bobble?